MW00929666

DEVIL'S GROUND
ARCO STATION

BY OAKLEY DEAN BALDWIN

Copyright © 2014 ODB Publishing

Check out my other stories and books at:

http://thebaldwinstories.wix.com/author-blog

We all go through things throughout our life time. Some things we just know are going to be exciting and different. Some of you who remember the show the Twilight Zone will closely relate to this story. The Twilight Zone is the best description.

Prologue

This book is a work of non-fiction, based on my personal experiences and historical facts that were available at the time of this writing; gathered from multiple sources that were pieced together into a plausible story.

With all the strange circumstances, events, and happenings, all the mayhem with accidents, injuries, deaths, suicide, and robbery have proven to be quite mysterious. Over the years, we have often wondered if the gas station ground was haunted, on Devils ground, or possibly an old unmarked Indian grave.

This family story surrounds a business that my father, Howard Baldwin, purchased in 1975.

The name of the business was B&S Arco gas station located at 2016 Harper Road at the Interstate 77 Bridge in Beckley, West Virginia. The station was located on the east side of the Check Mark Club just across the bridge.

The gas station was a cinder block and brick building with three work bays, an office area with snacks and drinks for sale along with two small bathrooms for customers.

We performed State Vehicle Inspections, minor engine repair, brake repair, tire repair and installation. We sold gas, oil, batteries, belts, hoses, tires, drinks and food goods.

I married Doris Gail Barber on July 17, 1975. Shortly after our wedding, my wife and I purchased the gas station from my father and operated it for about eighteen months.

The station came with a 12X65 foot mobile home which was directly behind the station. The gas station was registered with the Department of Employment Security as B&S Southern States Service Station.

When I first purchased the gas station, my father stayed on part-time for several months working the first four hours or so to open up in the mornings. He would open the station around 5:00 a.m. for the coal miners that had a long commute to their mines.

It was some of the hardest work I had ever endured with sixteen hour days, six and a half days a week. After standing on concrete floors for sixteen hours, I remember my legs and calf muscles would ache most of the night while trying to fall asleep.

During the time that we owned the station, I employed mechanics Jack Reeves, Ronnie Stover, Mike Endreson, and Norman Bennett Jr., AKA Jr..

It was a long, long eighteen months and the following stories are true and actual happenings.

TABLE OF CONTENTS

Part One
So it Began...

Needing to fill my gas tank, I pulled into the Arco gas station at 2016 Harper Road in Beckley, West Virginia in early 1975. My father and I were regular customers there and the station offered the cheapest fuel in town. While paying for my fuel, I noticed out the corner of my eye, a car rolling backwards and slamming into two parked cars and then coming to a stop.

The station's owner left the vehicle running and his ten year old son jumped in the front seat and pulled the vehicle in reverse. One could certainly say that turned out to be a costly mistake. Fortunately, no one was injured and all the damages could be repaired.

This accident happened right before my father purchased this gas station. I started to feel some bad luck had surrounded the Arco station on Harper Road.

As you will soon see, little did I know at the time that this accident was just the beginning of the mayhem to come and engulf quite a few of us. Were they accidental circumstances, coincidences or do we really know?

PART TWO
EXIT 3 SIGN ACCIDENT

On a cold West Virginia morning around 5:30 a.m., I was standing out in the misty rain filling up a portable propane tank on the west side of the station. My eyes caught the headlights of a car coming from under the 77 bridge traveling north bound towards Charleston. It was still dark outside and like a moth to a flame I was hypnotized by the headlights illuminating the roadway.

My eyes followed the car about seventy five yards and just as soon as the car passed the station property, it suddenly veered off the roadway and struck the large highway 77, Exit 3 sign. The eight-foot sign was completely mowed flat by the car.

The sound of the collision with these heavy metal sign posts was so loud it must have reverberated around the concrete walls of the gas station a half dozen times.

I immediately stopped what I was doing and ran as fast as I could towards the car. I remember thinking to myself, "this person has to be hurt, and he never applied his brakes."

Much to my surprise, the driver stepped out from the heavily damaged car and appeared uninjured. I got close enough to shine my flash light in his face and he just stared at me with the most blank and stoic look. Thinking he was in shock, I called out to him asking was he okay but he just got back into the car and drove off into the dark.

The collision also caused damage to the undercarriage of the vehicle. Also, with the amount of lost oil and radiator fluid, how that car was still drivable will always be a mystery to me.

PART THREE
DEATH COMES

On May 24, 1976, there was a young man named James Rhodes working with a company to obtain drilling core samples for the upcoming state highway project at the west side of the station lot. The station lot was up about forty to fifty feet from Interstate 77 highway below.

Like several times before, James took his break and purchased a drink inside the station. He told my father he was looking forward to going home soon to see his kids. My father exchanged some other general conversation with James but recalls telling him right before he left, "James, I wouldn't back that equipment any further on that hill, it's too dangerous."

I remember vividly that the drilling rig did not have a top or a roll bar and I thought to myself on several occasions that I wouldn't operate this piece of equipment anywhere other than on flat ground.

Just after 9:00 a.m., I was standing about forty feet away from the rig arranging tires on the side of the building into our used tire rack. James walked out of the station office and climbed upon the drilling rig and started it up promptly. James put the rig in reverse and started back about another foot and that's when things went terribly wrong!

I can still see the fear and the shock on James's face, the rig was not stopping, it kept moving backwards; it felt like a minute, but it was only a second or two.

The rig slid backwards and tumbled end over end landing on top of him. As the rig was tumbling down the hill, it caused the dirt and grass to fly up into the air which made a hellish noise.

We all ran down the hill to the bottom but there was no helping him at this point. The tires on this rig looked to weigh a ton and the front tire was on his head. He was killed instantly.

The Raleigh Register Newspaper reported on May 25, 1976 as follows:

Illinois Man Turnpike Victim

An employee of the A. H. Inspection Testing Engineering Co., Killed Monday morning on the West Virginia Turnpike has been identified as James Rhodes, 29, of Champaign, Ill.

Rhodes was crushed to death at about 9:20am Monday when a well-drilling machine rolled over him. The accident occurred just south of the Beckley exit of the Turnpike. The body, first taken to Rose and Quesenberry Funeral Home in Beckley, was sent Monday night to a funeral home in Champaign.

PART FOUR
ATTEMPTED ROBBERY

The Turnpike Gulf Gas Station on Harper Road up the street from us had just been robbed by two men with a large butcher knife. They drove a dark colored pickup truck in their get-a-way.

The Beckley Post-Herald Newspaper reported August 4, 1976 as follows:

"Suspects Jailed in TP Robbery. Two suspects in the early Tuesday morning armed robbery of the Turnpike Gulf service station on Harper Road were apprehended quickly by state police. One of the suspects, William Fogg, 35, is a former inmate of the Beckley Work/Release Center.

He was serving time for grand larceny, reduced from another armed robbery charge. Thieves robbed the station of $209 using a large butcher knife. Two attendants at the station, Gary Bradley and Joe Meadows, told police that the two robbers entered the building early Tuesday and demanded money. Bradley said he handed over the cash when he saw the Knife. Donald and Fogg were taken before Magistrate Joe Rodriguez Tuesday morning. Both were remanded to jail in lieu of $5000 appearance bonds. "

Just a few days before this robbery, my father came in to the station about 4:15 a.m. to open up. He unlocked the front door and turned on the lights from the electric breaker box. As he turned around, a woman was standing there at the front door inside the office. He did not see or hear a vehicle pull up and it was just like she had formed right out of thin air or more like stepping out of a shadow.

The woman appeared to be in her mid-thirties. She had on a dark overcoat and a large floppy hat. Both of her hands were in her coat pockets, she told my father that she needed money. My father had a carry concealed permit and always carried a pistol in his jacket pocket. You see he was a Korean War Vet who was trapped behind enemy lines.

One time he was missing in action for several days. If you ever planned to assault or rob someone, he would be the worst target you could pick.

He slowly placed his right hand in his pocket and onto the handle grip of his pistol.

He asked her if she was there to rob him saying, "Because if you are, I have a pistol in my pocket and I will shoot you deader than a door knob. I killed many men in the Korean War and I will kill you if I have to without hesitating!" Her eyes became as big as silver dollars as she slowly turned and stepped outside without saying a word. My father watched her walking quickly in the dark to a truck parked across the street.

She jumped into the passenger side and the truck sped away. They didn't turn on their lights until they got about a quarter mile down the road.

Was this incident somehow related to the robbery that would occur just a few days later? We will never know but one thing is for sure, they picked the wrong person to attempt to rob.

PART FIVE
THE BLACK CLOUD

I feel this event was truly an unexplained phenomenon! On July 4, 1976, Doris and I decided to celebrate our Country's 200 Year Bicentennial Anniversary by cooking out dinner and setting off some fireworks. We cooked hotdogs and hamburgers with chips, baked beans, and cold drinks.

We celebrated our 200 years of freedom and independence by setting off dozens of fireworks and bottle rockets. We all had a great time pitching horseshoes and the fireworks were beautiful as well as very colorful.

It was just about sundown when I noticed the black smoke from all of the fireworks.

It was like a black cloud descended on us, just hanging over our heads. The smell of the powder and smoke was gone. But what made this situation so strange was you could see the wind blowing on the trees all around the station at a good pace.

Yet, the cloud of black smoke was not floating away with the wind. The sight of this phenomenon caused me to break out in a sweat, and the sweat on my forehead began to run down the bridge of my nose. It was truly a strange sight to see.

The cloud was stationary almost in a complete circle directly overhead above the property and it remained there until it got dark, over forty five minutes. It had become too dark to tell what time the cloud finally disappeared, but it was gone the next morning.

I had worked the North Carolina State Fair for over thirty years; they closed the fair with a fireworks display each evening at 9:45 p.m. This situation never happened during any of these displays. I have never seen anything like this before or since!

PART SIX
BLACKED OUT?

Out front of the station we had two gas pumps. One was for leaded gas and the other was for unleaded gas. While I was pumping gas at the front pump about six feet away, a white Chrysler New Port driven by Richard Amon careened into the gas pump behind me.

The crash was so loud that I thought this would surely be the death of me. However, other than scaring me nearly to death, I was physically unharmed.

Once the car struck the pumps, sparks went immediately flying. Because of the sparks and large amount of gasoline leaking around the car, my first thoughts were of a fire or explosion.

I jumped over some debris and ran to the emergency electric shut off switch inside the building.

The car driven by Mr. Amon was still in drive and the back tires were spinning, digging ruts in the asphalt. Smoke was rolling off the back tires and the tires were squealing as the engine was revving. I then ran to the car and turned off the ignition switch and placed the car in park.

My wife Doris, who was a nurse, just happened to be off from the hospital that day. Hearing the collision she ran around from our trailer to see what had happened. She immediately began to pull Mr. Amon away from the car as I was turning off the vehicle ignition.

Once at a safe distance, we stood in awe at the destruction that Mr. Amon had caused. The gas pump was lying completely flat on the ground.

The top shelter post was damaged and the dinosaur on top of the shelter was about to fall over at any moment. The dinosaur was about ten feet long and six feet wide.

Mr. Amon was transported to the hospital by emergency services. Shortly after the accident, the family of Mr. Amon came and picked up his car and drove it home.

The next afternoon Mr. Amon came back to the station to thank us for pulling him out of his car. We walked around to the front of the station so he could inspect the damage.

We stopped at the pumps; Mr. Amon lit a cigarette and took a long drag on it. My wife at once said, "Please put that cigarette out, you could have killed my husband yesterday now you are going to blow us off of the map and they never will find our bodies!"

He quickly put out the cigarette and said he was sorry for lighting it. He stated he was still shaken up and had forgotten about the open pipes to the underground gasoline storage tanks which were directly under our feet.

The Raleigh County Register Newspaper reported the accident on August 28, 1976 as follows:

Dino Leans after Wreck, "Dino" the dinosaur leans precariously at the B&S Arco service station at 2016 Harper Road. The shelter supports were struck Saturday after-noon by a car driven by Richard J. Amon of 213 Summit drive, Beckley. Trp. C.R. Smithers of the Beckley State police said Amon blacked out at the wheel for no apparent reason. A gasoline pump was also knocked down in the accident, although no fire resulted. Two nurses on the scene, Mrs. Doris Baldwin and Miss Jackie W. Bethijian, pulled the unconscious Amon from his car. Amon's auto sustained minor body damage. (Raleigh Register Photo By John Anderson)

Part Seven
Death Returns...

The Mr. Amon car accident happened on
Saturday, August 27, 1976. On the
following Monday, the Arco Company
sent a repair mechanic to remove and
replace the damaged gasoline pump to get
us back up and running for business.

The repair mechanic pulled his truck
beside the pump and started working on
the damage. After a few minutes, he
backed his truck up to the edge of the
parking lot about fifty feet from his work
area and just barely out of view from the
office window. With little to do during
this time, I began to notice about every
fifteen minutes or so the mechanic would
go back to his truck.

First, I thought to myself he was rummaging through his hand tools but then he would return empty handed.

He wasn't getting much work done and after about ten trips back to his truck, I decided to get to the bottom of what was happening. Much to my surprise once at his truck, he would take a drink of Kaopectate and follow it with a drink of liquor.

This went on most of the morning, at least a half dozen or more times. I am not sure what the exact number of drinks he had was but it proved to be one too many. While walking back to the pumps from his truck, he suddenly fell over dead in the parking lot.

At that moment, I ran over to him and checked his vital signs which I was unable to find. We called the rescue squad which took around fifteen minutes to arrive. Even though we performed CPR on the mechanic the entire time, he was long dead once they arrived.

Part Eight
Escaped Prisoners

One afternoon near closing time, we had four or five Beckley City Police and Raleigh County Sheriff Deputies pull up with their blue and red lights activated to the side and rear of the station. They began searching the woods behind our mobile home.

They said they were looking for three escaped prisoners. They brought in the K9 units and you could hear the dogs barking and working about a half mile away into the surrounding woods.

About an hour or so later, several officers captured the three escaped prisoners and walked them out of the woods directly behind the gas station.

They still had their prison clothes on and appeared to be in dire straits. The escapees were dirty, muddy, and wet.

Maybe it was the long cold night or maybe it was the dogs and police that had found them that caused them to look this way. You could tell they had been on the run for some time.

They came out of the woods twenty feet from the front door of our mobile home. This was frightening to think about how if they had not been caught, my beautiful wife could have been inside there sleeping.

Part Nine
Horse Head

As I mentioned, we lived in a single wide mobile home directly behind the gas station. On Sundays, I would close the station around 4:00 p.m. and spend my only afternoon off with my wife. Doris would routinely pick up extra shifts to help make ends meet but kept Sunday afternoons free. After all, we were newlyweds!

At the time of my ownership of the gas station, there was an Animal Hospital next door. We would routinely get "escapees" dogs and cats that would show up around the pumps or in the mechanic bays. One Sunday after I had closed up shop and walked around to the mobile home, I laid down for a quick power nap.

This was a warm sunny afternoon and I had opened my windows to get some fresh air circulating through the home.

I remember lying in my bed with my eyes closed first hearing a noise like heavy breathing and naturally thought I was dreaming. I heard this noise three or four more times. I was not dreaming, it was more like a nightmare! I opened my eyes to see a large horse's head with huge snorting nostrils and big dark black eyes staring six inches from my face.

To say the horse's head in my window scared me would have been an understatement! I yelled and then sprang from my bed which scared the crap out of the horse. Thus, this caused it to very quickly pull his head back out of my window yanking the curtains and rods out the window with him.

He took off running down my driveway with my curtains around his head. It looked as though he was wearing a cape; we finally caught him about one hundred yards away still wearing our curtains.

PART TEN
SUPER BIRD ACCIDENT

The son of the owner of the Exxon station across the street owned a beautiful Blue 1970 Plymouth Super Bird. It was the one with the cone on the front and large fin on the rear.

He was always speeding up and down the road in that muscle car. One day he was showing off doing burn outs in my parking lot, when suddenly he left my lot wide open and the "pedal to the metal." I mean that car was screaming and he crossed the street and collided with his father's gasoline pump in front of the Exxon station, knocking the pump right over in the process. Even though this technically wasn't an Arco station incident, it had originated in my station's lot.

His father was so mad at him that he made him sell the Super Bird. Selling the Super Bird was a big mistake; today this car would be valued at over a half million dollars. There would be another story starting from the Exxon station later in this book.

PART ELEVEN
LET ME OUT OF HERE!

The following occurrence was not a tragedy but still a very weird happening. One afternoon a man drove up to the door near the office and I stepped out and asked him if I could help him. He started to ask me for directions to get to Charleston, and I heard someone say, "Let me out of here."

The man continued to tell me about how he had made a wrong turn several streets back. Then I heard it again, "Let me out of here." I said, "Did you hear that?" He said, "Hear what?" I said, "Someone is in your trunk!" He said, "That's crazy." Then I heard it again! Fearing the worst case scenario, I demanded that the man open his trunk. He said, "You want to see what?"

Overcome with anxiety, I then told him, "You are going to open your trunk, or I will call the police." He responded loudly, "Okay, be cool."

He walked over and opened the trunk but no "person" was there. There was something in there; however, it was a scary looking stage dummy that a ventriloquist would use. This dummy was truly scary, like one used in a horror movie.

Then he started laughing at the puzzled look on my face and said, "Let me out of here." Realizing he was throwing his voice and playing a prank on me, I said sarcastically, "That's real funny!" I never once saw his lips move and still today don't know how he did it, but he sure fooled me.

PART TWELVE
FLAME ON

One day while I was pumping gas for a customer I looked across the street at the Exxon Station. Suddenly, their bay door opened and I saw a man on fire. I'm not talking about his sleeve or his pants either. I'm talking about the type of on fire that looked like a fire demon was wrapped around his whole body! The flames had completely engulfed him and he was running straight for me. This boy was knocked kneed and pigeon-toed but was running like a bolt of lightning.

He ran across Harper Road and just missed getting hit by a passing car. He continued towards me so I abruptly stopped pumping the gas and met him about ten feet from the gas pumps.

I grabbed him by his wrist and threw him to the ground, quickly pouring water from the plastic water container (which we kept at the pumps to fill up radiators) to put out the fire.

Most of his hair was burnt off, his pants and shirt were burnt off, and the skin on his arms was hanging like string cheese. He was growling and trying to catch his breath from his injured lungs. It was one of the most grotesque things I had ever seen and the smell of skin burning and smoldering is something you don't forget.

Jack Reeves and I loaded him into Jack's car and drove him to the local hospital. He spent a long time in the hospital receiving skin grafts and care. I remember visiting him about a half dozen times.

He told me during one of my visits that he was cleaning up with some paint thinner and must have hit a light bulb with his broom handle and caused a spark to start the fire.

He didn't know why he ran over to me from across the street. I asked him one day and he said something was pulling him my way and he was running as hard as he could. This accident was also before the national awareness campaign of stop, drop, and roll. Running while on fire is the last thing you should ever do.

His statement about something pulling him my way or over to the Arco gas station has always stuck with me as sounding very strange!

Part Thirteen
Men in Black

I hired a young man named Junior (Jr.) Bennett as a mechanic; he was a good mechanic, friendly, and a dependable employee.

Jr. had been with me about two months when a black car pulled up to the gas station office door. I was sitting in the office when three men in black dress suits jumped out of the car very quickly. One of the men grabbed Jr. and not being sure what was happening I yelled at them to stop and let him go. They told me they were Military Police Officers (MPs) and showed me their badges. They had come to arrest Jr. for being absent without leave AKA AWOL from the Army.

They must have had a picture of him because they didn't even ask him his name. They stated they were taking him to Fort Dix in New Jersey to process his time in jail.

Then, they quickly ushered him into their black car and sped away.

We were all shocked and confused as we didn't even know Jr. had joined the Army. He was only about nineteen years old at the time of his arrest.

Once he returned home from his thirty days in the brig at Ft Dix, I hired Jr. again as a mechanic and told him I would give him another chance.

PART FOURTEEN
TIRE CHANGE INCIDENT

One duty of a mechanic was to change and replace truck split ring tires. This was a dangerous operation. Once the tire was deflated, you very carefully beat the side of the tire with a large sledge hammer with a flat tip, freeing the side wall from the rim. At this point, you could remove the split ring, the rim, and inner tube from the tire.

You placed the new tire and inner tube over the rim and then placed the split ring around the rim. Blowing up and inflating the split ring tire was the most dangerous part of the operation; we always used a safety metal cage about four feet high and two feet wide for this process.

The tire was placed in the cage for protection in case the split ring blows off while adding air to the tire. The metal bars on the cage were designed to hopefully stop the ring.

One day Jr. Bennett was adding air to a split ring tire without the tire being in the safety metal cage. This action was totally against my safety policy.

The tire and split ring were facing up on the tire changer. While adding the air, the tire popped and blew off the split ring sending it to the ceiling of the garage with great force. The ring bounced off the ceiling and back down striking Jr. in the arm. He was very lucky because he avoided a serious injury and walked away with only a bruised forearm.

PART FIFTEEN
THE TRANCE

Jr. had worked with me for over half a year at this time. In all this time, he had always treated customers with respect and conducted himself professionally. But something strange happened this day out of the blue.

Jr. repaired a customer's car and then refused to get out of it. He locked the doors and just sat there behind the wheel as if he was in a trance.

The customer had already paid the bill and was ready to leave. I asked Jr. about a dozen times to please unlock the door and get out so the customer could go home. I tried knocking on the window but nothing I did would break his stare.

Jr. didn't appear to be mad but had an eerie, blank silent stare on his face with his hands gripping the steering wheel.

I called his parents by phone but no one answered. Eventually, after about an hour, he unlocked the car door and stepped out of the vehicle.

As a result of his actions, I questioned him on what was going on exactly. He would not tell me anything except he had some issues that he was working out for himself. It was almost closing time and I wouldn't let him work anymore that day. Jr. suddenly said, "I quit" without any more explanation.

That was the last time I saw Jr. in person, as his father came and picked up his last check the following week.

Although, I did hear from him some time later, Jr. called me on the phone and asked me for a reference to get a job in the coal mines near his home.

I remember telling the folks at the mines that he was a hard worker and dependable. They asked me about his AWOL from the Army and I told them that I over looked that because he was helping to support his family.

PART SIXTEEN
SUICIDE OR MURDER

Not long after I sold the gas station, I heard that Jr. committed suicide while working at the coal mines.

At the time I received the news, I thought he was working as a coal miner but later his father told me he was hired as a security officer. I am not sure if security officers carried weapons on the mine property or not, but evidently Jr. had a weapon with him at the time of this death.

On the contrary to the suicide statements, Junior's father insisted that he would not have taken his own life and suggested that someone had murdered him.

Jr. was a good man. I personally don't know what happened; I only know he was always soft spoken and kind hearted. In addition, he appeared to be a very good brother to his siblings. His brothers and sisters would come to the gas station almost every day with their father to drop him off and pick him up.

One can only believe that his death was properly investigated by the authorities when the tragedy happened.

I ran into Jr.'s father three or four more times over the next few months. Each time he shared with me how disappointed he was with the suicide investigation, insisting it was a murder. I reminded him about the time that Jr. refused to get out of the car while working with me, but he said that had nothing to do with it.

PART SEVENTEEN
THE STRIKE

We had open credit book accounts for over one hundred customers and most of them were coal miners. They would purchase gas and food goods, sign their credit book, and pay their account at the end of each month.

In 1977, many miners got laid off from work or they went on strike. As a result, I carried my credit on customers' purchases as long as I could for many months. I tried to collect what was due but because they were not working they couldn't or simply wouldn't pay their bills.

After the strike was over, most of the miners paid what they could but some never came back and the credit accounts were not paid.

This loss of money, along with the long hours and stressful events, caused me to put the business up for sale. We sold the business back to the prior owner, Bobby Acord. Now that I think about it I never saw him at the station during the time I operated it. He didn't live far away but as soon as I put the station up for sale he just kind of showed up.

I told him about some of the strange happenings. Bobby was very stoic about the events that I shared with him. It was almost like he didn't believe me.

As far as I can remember, he ran the business until the State took the property for the Interstate 77 interchange. Later, they built a Super 8 Motel on the property.

Unfortunately, as you will see, the tragic and strange happenings still continued …. Like a loaded, speeding freight train applying its brakes trying to come to a sudden stop!

PART EIGHTEEN
THE GREATEST HEARTBREAK

In the fall of 1977 before we sold the station, Doris was about three months pregnant with our son, Roy Dean.

During a visit with her father Roy Charles Barber, she started to notice his skin was yellowing. Worried about him, she followed him around on his bread truck route, and stopped him at one of his stores that he supplied bread to regularly. She insisted that he needed to see the doctor about his skin and eyes turning yellow.

A few days later she followed up by taking him to his MD appointment. At only fifty four years old, they discovered that he had terminal liver cancer.

Her father (and my father-in-law) was the greatest man I ever knew. He walked the Christian life every day. He always made you feel that you were the most important person in his life.

He lit up the room everywhere he went, and with Roy it was always about Jesus. He was so humble and giving. In my entire life, no man walked closer to Jesus than Roy Charles Barber.

Over the next two years, Roy was in and out of the hospital several times. During one of Roy's stays, my youngest brother (at thirteen years of age) skipped school three times to stay all day with Roy at the hospital. Roy always made a positive impression on everyone who interacted with him.

PART NINETEEN
RESTART OF ASPLUNDH TRUCKS

On the property we had an agreement with a local tree cutting Service Company by the name of Asplundh Tree Company giving them permission to park their trucks and chipping equipment around the back and sides of the gas station in the evenings after work.

In return for this free parking they would purchase all of the fuel for their trucks and chipping equipment each day from us. There were six large trucks each pulling a chipper with very large fuel tanks. The two and three man crews from each truck would also purchase food, drinks, coffee, etc. from inside the station lobby.

During the winter months, crews would come in early to start the trucks so the engines would warm up especially on the extra cold mornings. This particular extra cold morning something happened which none of us could explain.

All of the trucks and chippers failed to start, the engines would turn over but they would not fire and run. We assessed the problem by process of elimination. The batteries were charged and functional with the terminals being clean and showing no shows of corrosion.

Once we attached a battery charger to the batteries and sprayed ether into the carburetors, after several hours, each truck and chipper engine finally did start up.

You might think, well it was a cold morning after all maybe the batteries were weak? Well, over half of the batteries were less than a year old, almost new.

All of trucks were locked and the fuel tanks had locking caps. All the other vehicles on the lot started right up, so it couldn't be the cold weather and no other employee or customer for that matter that was asked that day had any problems starting their vehicles.

Everyone there kept saying they never heard of anything like this happening before. It was just another day in the Twilight Zone called the B&S Arco.

PART TWENTY
TAX MAN COMETH

In the spring of 1978, just after I sold the Gas station, Doris was contacted by an IRS agent about back taxes on the gas station.

Doris was pregnant with our son Roy Dean at this time and the bad news of back taxes and fines caused her to become very upset.

I was working with a local plumbing company. We didn't have cell phones back in those days and my supervisor had to come all the way out to my job just to ask me to call my wife at home as soon as possible.

Once I arrived at the nearest pay phone booth, I called Doris and she informed me that we owed back taxes and could be fined and put in jail.

To say she was very upset would have been an understatement! To the contrary, I explained we had a book keeper and paid quarterly taxes and should not owe any back taxes.

I took the extra steps to ensure we paid all of our taxes and paid them on time regularly.

That afternoon when I met with the IRS agent, he explained that we owed back taxes at the gas station and we would have to pay them plus a fine or could face jail time.

He stated the taxes from 1972 needed to be paid immediately. I asked him if he could to repeat the year; he took several minutes looking through his paperwork and stated the year 1972 again. I told him, are you sure you have the right gas station, we were in high school in 1972, and didn't purchase the gas station until 1975.

The agent then toiled through his papers for a couple more minutes; he then looked up at me and said he was sorry, very sorry! We never heard anything else from this gentleman.

PART TWENTY ONE
INTERSTATE 81 DEATHS BY FIRE

Even though I sold the property, the mayhem continued. Bobby Acord worked along with his father James at the gas station. His father was in his late sixties, but he still worked full time as a mechanic for Bobby.

On October 21, 1978, both of Bobby's parents James and Nana Belle were killed in a car accident. I was told they were driving the wrong way on Interstate 81 in Virginia. The cars burst into flames killing both James and Nana and both people in the other car.

The Charleston Gazette newspaper reported as follows: Oct. 24, 1978, Beckley Couple's Service Wednesday.

BECKLEY -- Joint service will be 1 p.m. Wednesday for James Clayton Acord, 66 and his wife, Nana Belle Acord, 58, of Route 4, Beckley, who were killed Saturday in an automobile accident on Interstate 81 in Christiansburg, Va.

I never saw or heard from Bobby again after we sold the station back to him and we had moved away. But I sometimes wondered if he thought about all those strange happenings that I shared with him once he received the news of his parent's fatal accident.

About the same time of this accident, late summer of 1978 while at the State Police Academy, I experienced a very weird occurrence.

As a cadet we all had to be certified as Emergency Medical Technicians (EMTs) as part of our twenty-four weeks of training. We had to work several shifts at the City of Charleston Hospital in Kanawha County, West Virginia. We also had to witness several autopsy procedures. One procedure was to examine a body after death to determine the cause of death or the character and extent of changes produced by disease or injuries.

I was very nervous about the thought of witnessing an autopsy; they called it a postmortem examination.

The Instructors loaded us cadets into several vans and we were driven over to the Coroner's Office in Charleston.

Once we arrived, staff led us into what appeared to be an operating room. There in the middle of the room was a deceased man lying on a steel table. It was very cold and quiet. My wedding ring became loose and I could feel it slip down my finger.

I was the first cadet to enter the room; the Coroner welcomed us and told us to gather around him at the table. I really did not want to look at this man, but I was two feet away from his head. It was obvious to me that he had been involved in a terrible accident.

I thought this is someone's child, husband and or father. I said a quiet silent prayer for his family.

The Coroner started the procedure and was explaining the processes when I noticed that this man looked familiar to me. Somewhere in my brain I recognized this gentleman.

I started to feel light headed and sick with the fear that I may know this man. He looked like a man who had come by the ARCO station each week for fuel.

Could this be Mr. Reagan? My sister was very good friends with Mr. Reagan's daughter. They were friends in school and would have sleep overs at Mr. Reagan's home on Dry Hill road in Beckley.

Through the crowd of fellow cadets, I made my way slowly down to his feet. There was a tag on his big toe but I couldn't read the name, it was on the back side of the tag. I took a deep breath and reached for the tag, turned it over.............

The name written on the tag was Reagan. I swallowed hard and prayed again, this time for my sister by name.

PART TWENTY TWO
INTERSTATE 81 FAMILY
DEATHS

On November 26, 1978, just over a month after the fatal car accident of Mr. and Mrs. Acord on Interstate 81 in Virginia, I received word on my job to call my mother at home.

It was lunch time and we were eating at the Pinnacle Drive Inn in Pineville, West Virginia; the owner allowed me to use their phone in the back room to call mom in Beckley. There was no answer the first time I called. However, once she answered, she was crying so hard I could barely understand what she was trying to tell me.

She finally managed to tell me that her brother Hobert and his wife Stella were just killed in a car accident on Interstate 81 in Virginia.

I could feel my knees buckle some and my eyes started to water as the warm tears started down the side of my face.

I tried to pray with mom on the phone, but all I could say was "Lord, please send mom the comforter." In uniform with a room full of Wyoming County citizens and two other State Troopers, I had to quickly wipe away the tears and compose myself.

Hobert was a pastor in Baltimore, Maryland. He was a true man of God and had a wonderful witness. Stella was beautiful and kind.

I don't believe my mother ever got over this accident. Her personality dramatically changed from always being happy to always being stoic. Mom terribly missed her brother Hobert until the day she died; emotionally, she was never the same. It turned out these two separate accidents were right down the road from each other on Interstate 81.

Allowing my mind to drift back and seriously think about this period of time in my life, I have had mixed feelings about the dark challenges and suffering that enveloped this piece of land!

With all the numerous circumstantial suffering, strange events, and happenings, the question must be asked: Was the gas station ground haunted, on Devils ground, or possibly an old unmarked Indian grave?

Some say there is an old Indian Curse on West Virginia near the Kanawha River because of the cold blooded murder of Chief Keigh Tugh Quah Cornstalk.

During the American Revolution, Indian Chief Keigh Tugh Quah Cornstalk worked to keep the Shawnee neutral, representing his people during treaty councils at Fort Pitt in 1775 and 1776. When the British attempted to build a coalition of Indians to fight against the colonists, Chief Cornstalk refused to join with them.

Many Shawnees hoped to take advantage of the war and use the British to aid them in their efforts to reclaim lands lost to the colonists. In the fall of 1777 , Chief Cornstalk and a small party made a diplomatic visit to the American Fort Randolph.

Chief Cornstalk and his two companions were detained by fort commander Captain Arbuckle. Captain Arbuckle decided on his own initiative to take the Shawnees hostage.

During this hostage ordeal, outside of the fort, while hunting, two young soldiers were fired upon and one was killed, when his bloody corpse was returned to the fort, the soldiers in the garrison were enraged. Acting against orders, they broke into the quarters where Chief Cornstalk and the other Indians were being held.

This group of man blamed Chief Cornstalk's son, Elinipsico for the killing, who had come to check on his father. Elinipsico denied the charge, but Chief Cornstalk, his men, and his son, were summarily shot to death.

As the soldiers burst through the doorway, Chief Cornstalk rose to meet them. It was said that he stood facing the soldiers with such bravery that they paused momentarily in their attack.

This gesture of respect wasn't enough though and the soldiers opened fire with their muskets. One tried to escape up through the chimney but was pulled back down and slaughtered. Ellinipisico was shot where he had been sitting on a stool. As for Chief Cornstalk, he was shot eight times before he fell to the floor.

As he laid there dying in the smoke-filled room, he was said to have pronounced his now legendary curse. He looked upon his assassins and spoke to them the following: "I was the border man's friend.

Many times I have saved him and his people from harm. I never warred with you, but only to protect our wigwams and lands.

I refused to join your paleface enemies with the red coats. I came to the fort as your friend and you murdered me. You have murdered by my side, my young son.... For this, may the curse of the Great Spirit rest upon this land. May it be blighted by nature, may it even be blighted in its hopes, and may the strength of its peoples be paralyzed by the stain of our blood."

American leaders were thoroughly alarmed by the murder of Chief Cornstalk who they believed was their only hope of a Shawnee neutrality treaty.

Governor Patrick Henry demanded Chief Cornstalk's killers be brought to trial, but no one was arrested and the militiamen who perpetrated the murders were shortly ordered to return home. Subsequently, some inquiries into the murderers were made, but no action was ever taken.

The bodies of the other Indians were then taken and dumped into the Kanawha River but Chief Cornstalk's corpse was buried near the fort on Point Pleasant grounds. Here he remained for many years, but he would not rest in peace. In 1840 street builders unearthed his grave, placed his remains in a metal box and carved his name on the box. They moved his remains to the Mason County courthouse grounds.

With the building of the new Mason County Courthouse the decision was made to move his grave to the historical Tu-Endie-Wei Park in 1954 at the junction of Ohio and Kanawha Rivers.

These cold blooded murders were a traumatic moment in time. The murder of these men turned the Shawnees from a neutral people into the most implacable warriors, who raided Virginia, now West Virginia settlements for the next twenty five years after the incident.

The Kanawha River drains into the New River which runs into Raleigh County where Beckley is the capital seat of Raleigh County.

Some say traumatic moments in time can leave an indelible impression on a building or area like a residual haunting. Residual haunting activities can occur when something traumatic occurs like a murder or death. They say that negative energy is blasted into the atmosphere, causing an imprint or record of the event.

These events can play out over and over again. It is said there is no interaction between you and the entity.

I never saw or heard anything from an entity, solitary essences or a ghost, but I do believe in the spirit world.

I take comfort with the following statement by Martin Luther King, Jr:

"I believe that unarmed truth and unconditional love will have the final word in reality. This is why right, temporarily defeated, is stronger than evil triumphant."

In the aftermath, I can say that some of our natural suffering we cause all by ourselves, and sometimes it is caused by the actions of evil men.

But circumstantial suffering is caused from being in the wrong place at the wrong time; I don't feel there is any point trying to find out the reason why, because sometimes bad things just happen. One thing is for sure.... we were very glad to sell the business and move away.

(Thank God!) The End

Sources

Personal Experiences

The Raleigh Register Newspaper May 25, 1976

The Beckley Post-Herald Newspaper August 4, 1976

The Raleigh County Register Newspaper August 28, 1976

The Charleston Gazette Newspaper October 24, 1978

Statement by: Martin Luther King, Jr.

ACKNOWLEDGMENTS

To my wife Doris Gail Barber Baldwin, whose love and giving support make all things possible. A true Proverbs 31: 10-31 wife.

To my son Roy Dean Baldwin, and my daughter Amanda Baldwin, many thanks for your long hours and hard work.

To my friend Daniel Quinn Woolard for your hard editing work.

To my friend Brandon Kloecker for formatting and editing.

Check out my other stories and books at:

http://thebaldwinstories.wix.com/author-blog

Contact email:
thebaldwinstories@gmail.com

Please remember to write an online review for me.

Also, check me out on Facebook at:

https://www.facebook.com/The-Baldwin-Stories

Made in the USA
Columbia, SC
08 April 2018